A ROOKIE READER®

WHAT'S IN A BOX?

By Kelly Boivin

Illustrated by Janice Skivington

Prepared under the direction of Robert Hillerich, Ph.D.

CHILDRENS PRESS®

CHICAGO

Library of Congress Cataloging-in-Publication Data

Boivin, Kelly.
    What's in a box? / by Kelly Boivin ; illustrated by
Janice Skivington.
       p. cm. — (A Rookie reader)
    Summary: Describes, in verse, different types of
boxes and what they may hold.
    ISBN 0-516-02010-2
    [1. Boxes—Fiction. 2. Stories in rhyme.]
    I. Skivington, Janice, ill. II. Title. III. Series.
PZ8.3.B5999Wg 1991
[E]—dc20   91-4062
                                      CIP
                                      AC

What's in a box?

What kind of box?

There is sand in a sandbox

and shoes in a shoe box,

mail in a mailbox,

and tools in a toolbox.

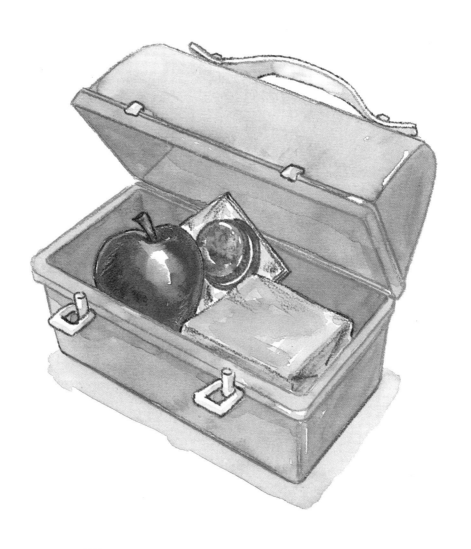

There is lunch in a lunch box,

and music in a music box,

toys in a toy box,

and jewels in a jewel box.

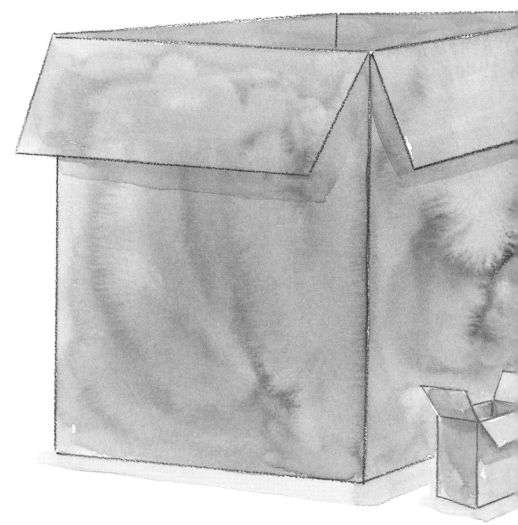

Big boxes, small boxes,

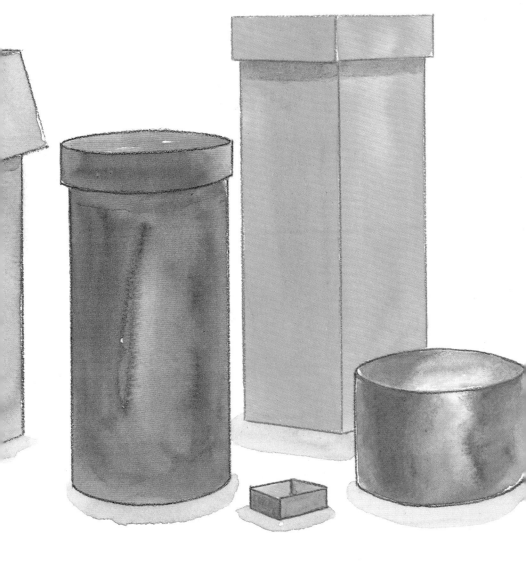

round boxes, tall boxes.

Boxes for crayons,

boxes for hats,

19

boxes for cookies,

and boxes for cats.

There are jack-in-the-boxes,

stacking boxes,

24

and great big moving
van packing boxes.

Boxes with ribbons, boxes with bows,

boxes of tissue ACHOO! for your nose.

Boxes for squashes
and boxes for squids.

But . . . who has the most
fun with boxes?

KIDS!

WORD LIST

			stacking
a	great	moving	tall
achoo	has	music	the
and	hats	nose	there
are	in	of	tissue
big	is	packing	toolbox
bows	jack-in-the-boxes	ribbons	tools
box	jewel	round	toy
boxes	jewels	sand	toys
but	kids	sandbox	van
cats	kind	shoe	what
cookies	lunch	shoes	what's
crayons	mail	small	who
for	mailbox	squashes	with
fun	most	squids	your

About the Author

Kelly Boivin lives in Maine with her husband, two children, two enormous dogs, and a tiger cat. They all live in semi-chaos in a hundred year old house, where things fall apart a lot more often than they get put together.

Kelly spends her days playing with blocks and finger paint as a Head Start preschool teacher, and she enjoys it very much, because she gets a lot of hugs and kisses and all the graham crackers she can eat.

She enjoys reading, cross-country skiing, camping at the beach, and, of course, writing.

Kelly also wrote *Where Is Mittens*, another Rookie Reader.

About the Artist

Janice Skivington lives in Wheaton, Illinois, with her husband Jay and their children Adam, Diana, and Gillian. The artwork for this book was a family effort as the children, their friends, and the family cat, Morris, all took a turn posing for the drawings.